For Isabel, the gentle, adventurous one

www.dragonbloodpirates.co.uk

ORCHARD BOOKS
338 Euston Road, London NW1 3BH

First published in 2008 by Lothian Children's Books,
an imprint of Hachette Livre Australia
First published in the UK in 2011 by Orchard Books

ISBN 978 1 40830 827 1

Text © Dan Jerris 2009
Skull, crossbones and ragged parchment image © Brendon De Suza
Map illustrations on pages 4–5 © Rory Walker, 2008
All other illustrations © Orchard Books 2011

A CIP catalogue record for this book is available from the British Library.

10 9 8 7 6 5 4 3 2 1

Printed in Great Britain

Orchard Books is a division of Hachette Children's Books,
an Hachette UK company.

www.hachette.co.uk

The Zombies' Treasure

Dan Jerris

ORCHARD BOOKS

Pirate Mateys and Scallywags

Alleric (Al) Breas: Lives in Drake Drive and owns a mysterious sea trunk that takes him to the Dragon Blood Islands

Blacktooth McGee: A very nasty pirate who runs the brigantine *The Revenge*

Demon Dan: An evil pirate who died on Dragon Island and whose black diamond became stuck between a dragon's teeth

Evil Pearl: A deathless pirate who becomes Queen of Pearl Island and sacrifices people to a sea monster

Flash Johnny: Blacktooth's devious and greedy cabin boy

Grandfather: Mahoot's grandfather and guardian of the swimming elephants on Sabre Island

Greeny Joe: A shark so big and old that mould grows on his skin, making him glow green in the dark

Grenda: Snotty Nell's daughter

Gunner: The pirate captain of the ship *The Invincible*

Halimeda (Hally) Breas: Al's younger sister

Mahoot: Captain Gunner's cabin boy

Mozzy: *The Invincible*'s bosun – small and fast

Jack Seabrook: Al's best friend

Pigface McNurt: Blacktooth's bosun; a huge pirate with a ring through his nose

Prince Alleric: The prince who once ruled Sabre Island but disappeared in mysterious circumstances

Princess Haree: The princess of Ruby Island

Razor Toe: A deathless pirate who has enslaved the people of Ruby Island

Sharkbait: Snotty Nell's one-legged bosun

Slicer: *The Invincible*'s cook

Snakeboot: A magical white three-legged cat with purple eyes. Legend has it he once belonged to a terrifying pirate called Vicious Victor.

Snotty Nell: A horrible one-eyed pirate who sails a worn-out Indiaman called *Nausi VIII*

Stanley Spong: A crooked, sneaky trader in town who cheats people

Vampire Zu: Snotty Nell's huge first mate

Velvetfoot: A fearsome pirate distinctive for his velvet shoes that let him creep up on his victims unannounced

Vicious Victor: A pirate ghost. He used to pillage the Dragon Blood Islands and stole the magical sabre and scabbard that belonged to Prince Alleric.

Return to the Dragon Blood Islands

"We've collected three black diamonds for the Scabbard of Invincibility," said Al Breas, holding up a silver sheath. "Now there's only one more to find before it will get legendary powers."

"Then, when you wear it, you'll be invincible," said Jack Seabrook, Al's best friend. "We need to go back to the

Dragon Blood Islands."

"Yep, I agree," said Al.

"Great! Are we going to take the Dragon Blood Sabre and scabbard this time?" asked Jack.

Al thought for a few moments before answering. "I'd rather not," he said. "If a pirate sees them we'll be in trouble, and I'm not invincible yet, just deathless." He shuddered slightly.

"Why don't we just take our chances?" said Jack, realising his friend was worried about it.

"I suppose," said Al. "I keep having horrible thoughts about wearing it. Like I'm alive but my head is missing, or my gizzards are ripped out and I have to try to stitch them back in. This whole deathless thing gives me the creeps. Who'd want to be like Razor Toe and Evil Pearl?"

"I'm not so keen on the deathless thing

either," Jack agreed. "They were horrible. Just thinking about them makes me want to vomit."

"I wonder where the final diamond is…" said Al. "Maybe there's some other ancient old pirate out there causing trouble?"

"Or it could be at the bottom of the sea so we'll never find it," said Jack with a chuckle. "I think we should just go back to have a bit of fun. I can't wait to see Mahoot and Gunner again."

"They're probably wondering how we disappeared from *The Invincible* so suddenly," said Al. "I'm sure Gunner thinks I used the Dragon Blood Sabre, and that we don't trust him."

"We could try telling him the truth," said Jack, hesitantly.

"Let's get changed then, and see if we can find him," said Al. "Who knows, we might end up on Sabre Island and go swimming with the elephants again," Jack said with a sparkle in his eyes.

Several minutes later the boys were dressed in their pirate clothes, ready to leave the twenty-first century and Al's home at number five Drake Drive.

Al took a key from a hook, unlocked an old sea trunk that had a map of the Dragon Blood Islands painted on its base, and took a deep breath. As he stepped into the trunk a familiar tingling went up through his feet and carried to his fingers. He became transparent, the air glowed mysteriously and he vanished. Jack stepped in behind his friend, wondering where they would land this time.

The Warning Bell

Al and Jack had landed somewhere so dark they could barely see their hands in front of their eyes. A heaving swell under their feet and a heavy night sky above told them they were at sea, on a ship, but the eerie tolling of a bell confused them. Bells were usually found in churches, weren't they — not on the waves?

A pallid shape looming out of the dark near the boat's rails attracted their attention.

Al stepped closer and found himself staring into the empty eye sockets of a skull. "This isn't good," he whispered. "Not good at all."

More lifeless faces peered back at them from the walls of a small cabin. "There are skulls everywhere!" gulped Jack, the hairs rising on his neck.

"Let's keep away from the cabin," said Al. "Somebody nasty could be sleeping there. Let's move towards the bow."

The boys climbed down a stairway that led to an open hull fitted with rowing benches. "It's like a giant rowboat," said Jack, as they clambered over the oars.

"At least fifty people would be needed to row this ship," observed Al. "But it's empty. What's a rowing boat doing out in the middle of the ocean? And why does that bell keep ringing?"

"It's like a slave galley, but with no slaves," said Jack. "And there are more skulls nailed beside every set of oars."

"Maybe the ringing is a ship's bell," said Al hopefully. "If it's another ship nearby, we might be able to get off this spooky boat."

The boys stood on tiptoe and peered over the bowsprit into the night. Not far away a lantern shone from a small rowboat, illuminating a man rowing away from the galley. He moved purposefully towards a bell mounted on a raft. The bell tolled with each wave, and the boys realised it was warning of razor-sharp rocks jutting from the ocean.

"What's the guy in the dinghy doing?" asked Jack, as the man climbed onto the raft.

The ocean swell lifted the boys high and they lost vision for a minute. Seconds later the mighty bell rang again. When the raft came back into sight, a knife glinted as the man hacked the bell's supporting ropes. With a mighty clang the bell plunged into the waters.

"What did he do that for?" asked Jack.

"I guess we'll find out," said Al, "because he's heading back here."

"But we don't want him to find us!" said Jack. He tapped a grinning skull beside him. "I don't want to end up like that. We'd better hide, quickly."

It didn't take the boys long to find supply boxes covered with canvas, near the prow. Beside the boxes were several large water barrels, lashed against the hull, hiding a space made by the hull's wooden ribs. Al and Jack ducked behind the barrels, squeezing themselves into the gap with their backs against the wall. It was uncomfortable, but they had a line of sight all the way up the boat to the cabin.

A bump against the side of the ship and the slither of ropes told the boys the lone rower had returned – and he was lashing the rowboat to the galley.

Shipwreck

The day broke with a fresh wind that tossed the galley on its anchor. The man who had cut the bell from the raft sat cross-legged on the deck in front of his cabin.

Al squirmed in his hiding place, trying to make the blood move in his legs. He was wondering if he should crawl out and announce his presence – he could no longer stand the wood pressing into every part of his body. But suddenly the man stood up. He shuffled down the stairs and through the

rowing benches towards the water barrel.
Red velvet slippers muffled his footsteps.

With heavily jewelled hands he lifted the
lid of the water barrel, only inches from Al's
nose, and collected a cup hanging from a
string. "Arggh," he grunted, as he slurped the
water and licked his lips, "there'll be a storm
by nightfall." He chuckled and tapped a skull
nailed above the barrel. A gold ring with a
large black diamond flashed in
the sunlight. Al's heart lurched
in his chest at the sight.

"And so, old ship mate,"
the man continued,
addressing the skull.
"Ye'll be a-grinning,
'cause another capt'n
will be a-rowing in yer
old place soon enough.
For the storm'll bring
Velvetfoot a new crew.

And ye were a great old capt'n, were ye not!
Ye gave old Velvetfoot many a good treasure."
He chuckled, replaced the cup on the nail,
turned and went silently back to his cabin.

The sea rose higher, crashing onto the
nearby rocks, and the galley seesawed on its
anchor. The wind tossed darkening clouds,
and Al's legs cramped painfully.

"It's getting very rough," whispered Jack.
"I'm in agony. I can't stand it any longer.
I think I'd rather risk death."

"Wait!" Al pleaded. "I saw a black diamond
on the man's hand! It's too dangerous. Maybe
tonight, while he's sleeping, we can take his
rowboat and escape."

By night Al's stomach was grumbling with
hunger, his bottom was numb and a storm
was making conditions unbearable.

Finally, when it was late and no light came
from the cabin, he dared to make a move.

"Let's try to get out of here," he whispered
to Jack, as he dragged himself from his hiding
place and slithered out into the hull on his
stomach. Jack followed, pulling himself from
his hidey-hole.

They were lying on their backs, rubbing
their aching arms and legs, when a loud
bang! startled them into sitting up. The
strong wind brought a sickening crash of
wood grinding over rocks, the booming
of sails as they were backed in the wind and
then the shriek of tearing canvas. This was
followed by shouts of disbelief and fear from
men in danger of drowning.

"Someone's hit the rocks in the storm,"
said Al. "They'll sink! What'll we do?"

As if in answer, there was a flash of light
from Velvetfoot's cabin. Velvetfoot shuffled to
the rails, then to his dinghy, carrying a lantern
and a blunderbuss.

The boys raced to their vantage point

at the prow and watched as, in the raging spume of waves, a small trading boat was smashed against the reef.

Velvetfoot rowed towards the boat and waited till a longboat was lowered from it by ropes, which the crew would use to escape their sinking vessel. When the life-saving boat was halfway to the water, Velvetfoot fired his blunderbuss. The ropes burst apart, sending the longboat crashing into the turbulent sea.

Several men fell with it. Velvetfoot rowed towards one of the floundering men and hauled him from the water, before rowing him back to the galley.

Once aboard, Velvetfoot led the man, at the point of his blunderbuss, to the cabin. He brought out a dark blue bottle and ordered the survivor to drink.

Within seconds, the rescued man fell senseless to the deck. Velvetfoot rolled him to one side and returned to his dinghy.

The crew of the broken-backed trading boat stood miserably by the gunnels, gazing at the murderous sea slowly destroying their longboat – and their chance of escape.

Velvetfoot rowed towards the stricken vessel. "Throw old Velvetfoot a rope!" he called. "I'll save your hides, but Velvetfoot's rowboat can only carry one at a time. Have patience and Velvetfoot'll save you all!"

One at time, he brought the men to his

galley and urged them to drink, and by daybreak, more than fifty lay unconscious at the stern. Jack and Al could only watch in horror.

In the pre-dawn light the pirate skull and crossbones flew above the shredded sail of the wrecked trading boat. Jack and Al realised they knew this ship – and its captain! They soon saw the last man lowering himself into Velvetfoot's tossing dinghy. Sure enough, it was Blacktooth.

As soon as Blacktooth was in the boat, Velvetfoot ordered him to drink. Blacktooth swigged from the blue bottle and slumped forward.

"I don't think Velvetfoot knows who he's dealing with," whispered Jack. "When the pirates wake up they'll take over the galley. Velvetfoot can't fight them all."

"It's getting light," warned Al. "Velvetfoot might see us. We'd better hide, but let's take

some food from
the store first." He
lifted the canvas
and collected
some salty biscuits
from a barrel,
handing half to Jack.

"Starvation rations," said Jack, taking a
hungry bite.

The boys hurriedly climbed behind
the barrels and waited as an unconscious
Blacktooth was hauled up to the deck by
ropes. All they could do was wait.

Around midday one of the captured
pirates woke. Velvetfoot led him, unresisting,
to a rowing bench, saying, "Sit there, matey."

One by one, Blacktooth's pirates were
led like lambs to the galley benches. Pigface
McNurt, Blacktooth's bosun, was seated only
a metre from Al. Flash Johnny, Blacktooth's
cabin boy, was placed near the cabin on an

oar with another pirate. Al noticed that Flash was wearing a heavy yellow coat – he would be so hot if he was made to row!

Finally, Blacktooth was seated in the prow, not far from Al, who stared straight into his eyes, but the pirate looked back without a glimmer of recognition.

Velvetfoot weighed anchor and, at his command, Blacktooth and his men began rowing.

"What's wrong with them?" whispered Jack. "It's like they're dead, or sleepwalking."

"Like zombies," said Al. "It's as though they're not seeing anything around them at all."

The Zombie Crew

By late afternoon the pirate crew was still rowing. They hadn't stopped for a rest or for water. Finally, the ocean became calm and Velvetfoot ordered them to stop. They floated in the silent ocean, waiting in a shimmering heat haze.

As night arrived, a fog formed, swirling eerily around the galley. Velvetfoot collected his blue bottle and a basket filled with velvet slippers. As he passed each pirate, he made them take a drink. Then he removed their shoes and replaced them with slippers.

Blacktooth was the last to be given a drink from the bottle, and when the slippers were on his feet Velvetfoot sat down beside him.

"Matey, we're in a shippin' lane," Velvetfoot began. "Treasure and spices'll come this way on the current tonight. The fog'll be thick. Velvetfoot can do his best work, and ye'll help old Velvetfoot collect his reward. It'll be a rare treat for Velvetfoot to have another buccaneer to help with the chores." He chuckled and felt Blacktooth's bicep. "And ye

be a strong captain. It'll be weeks before your head sits with the others."

With those words, Velvetfoot left Blacktooth and went to the prow to stand watch. As the fog thickened, a heavy silence descended on the galley, made worse by Blacktooth's pirates sitting like dead men, without moving a muscle.

Eventually Velvetfoot said to himself, "There be a ship's light coming towards us. Now Velvetfoot must get to boarding it." He slipped silently past the boys and climbed

into his dinghy. Half an hour or more passed and he returned to the galley, holding the end of a rope. Following Velvetfoot's hand signals, several zombies began to heave on the rope. Then the gangplank was lowered and, one by one, the pirates disembarked.

Once everyone had left the galley, Al and Jack slid from their hiding place, guzzled water from the barrels and snatched more biscuits. Finally, they dared to climb to the rails to see what was going on.

Alongside the galley, only metres away, floated a galleon. Its lanterns reflected the mists, yet showed the decks clearly. Velvetfoot stood by the ship's wheel with several bodies at his feet.

"He must have sneaked on board," whispered Al. "He walks so quietly no one would have heard him. I think he's killed the crew on watch."

"Then he must have taken a rope and

pulled us alongside," said Jack. "Now I'll bet the zombies are going to rob the sleeping crew. No one will hear them walking in those velvet slippers."

"Could we get off?" asked Al. "Maybe we could climb aboard the galleon and raise the alarm?"

"Velvetfoot would see us. He can see the whole deck from where he's standing," said Jack. "And look, the zombies are coming back up from below with bundles of loot."

"They'll be back here any minute," said Al. "We'd better hide again. They've got to stow their booty somewhere. It won't all fit in that tiny cabin, and the deck's pretty small. Velvetfoot must have a place to put his treasure nearby. We might find a way to escape if he takes his loot somewhere else."

Velvetfoot's Cave

Once the treasure was stowed on board the
galley, Velvetfoot cast off from the galleon.
The boys saw a glimmer of flame light up
the sky and wondered if Velvetfoot had set
the ship alight before he left. They pitied the
poor crew.

The zombies rowed through the night,
and with the steady pull of the oars, Al and
Jack fell asleep, not waking until the sun
was high. They dared not move a muscle as
Velvetfoot was sitting with Blacktooth again,

chatting to him like an old friend.

"And that man over there," Velvetfoot was saying, pointing to a gold-toothed skull hanging on the other side of the hull, "he roamed the sea before your time and was Velvetfoot's seventieth captain. He gave a gold-filled frigate to Velvetfoot. He lasted one and a half moons before he stopped rowing. And Velvetfoot capped his teeth in gold as a reward. He smiles at Velvetfoot every day and the sun glints from his teeth. Ahh! It cheers Velvetfoot's heart. We had a grand time, that we did! And when you stop rowing, me hearty, I have a place for you and your one black tooth, near the prow."

Al shuddered at Velvetfoot's story, now understanding that the skulls decorating the galleon had once belonged to kidnapped captains.

Later that day the fog descended again, and the zombies rowed on through the night. In the morning Velvetfoot ordered the rowers to stop. He lowered the gangplank and, one by one, the zombies dropped their oars and unloaded the cargo from the ship.

When the galley was empty and silent, Al and Jack emerged from their hidey-hole, crept to the rails and discovered their boat was tied to a small jetty on an unknown island. It was their chance to escape! They climbed over the rails, raced down the jetty, and ran for the trees, where they hid.

When they were sure that Velvetfoot and the zombie pirates were far away, Jack and Al set out to explore. They soon found a banana tree to satisfy their hunger, and a bubbling stream to quench their thirst. As they crept along a jungle path they almost stumbled into the zombies, who were sitting, silent as the grave, beside a rocky overhang.

"Where's Velvetfoot?" whispered Jack, staring at the unmoving pirates.

"He can't be far away," Al replied. "If you look closely there's flattened grass where the zombies made a track carrying the treasure. It must be somewhere close by and they must be waiting for Velvetfoot to return."

"Weird," said Jack. "The track leads to that cliff, so there must be a cave around there."

"Or Velvetfoot has a tunnel or something

behind those trees," said Al. "It's hard to see from here."

"Do you think we should move further around?" asked Jack. "Or go back to the slave galley, steal Velvetfoot's dinghy and try to escape?"

"The zombie pirates will die if we don't help them," said Al. "They seem to need that potion to stay in a zombie state. And although Blacktooth and his pirates are the nastiest people ever, they're not half as bad as Velvetfoot. I don't know if we can just leave them to their fate and run away."

"If we could stop Velvetfoot from giving them that drink every day, I think they'd come to their senses," suggested Jack. "Perhaps we could try to destroy the potion?"

A strange series of clicks, coming from the cliff, interrupted their discussion. To their amazement a door the height and width of two men opened under the rocky overhang. Velvetfoot stepped out and clapped his hands loudly. The zombies stood to attention.

Velvetfoot disappeared behind some trees. There were several more clicks and the secret door shut with a dull thud.

Whistling a command, Velvetfoot walked back towards his boat, with the zombies following. The boys crept after them and watched as the zombies were marched up the gangplank and the slave galley cast off. Then they rowed away.

Now alone again on the island, Al and Jack decided to return to Velvetfoot's secret cave to try to work out how the door had opened. Al searched around the trees and found a set of seven large iron levers. He pushed one but it didn't move. But then he tried another and it *did* move, but when he tried a third, the second lever moved back to its original position.

"I think these levers are geared to move like the combination of a bank safe," said Al. "But finding the combination could take hours. Maybe we should try and get off this island before Velvetfoot comes back with more treasure."

"What's that?" said Jack suddenly. He was pointing to some letters scratched onto the

bark of the tree above Al's head:

ttwhorfeoeufriovnee

Al smiled. He was good at codes and this
one was easy. He pulled at a lever. It clicked
loudly. Then another. Within seconds he had
moved the seven levers in sequence and the
door in the cliff swung open.

Once inside, they found another set of levers with a similar code carved into the rock wall. This time it said:

Soenveetnhtrweoe

A large oil-filled lantern and a flint sat beside the levers. Al lit the lamp, pulled the levers and, with a series of loud clicks, the door slammed shut.

The boys walked along a tunnel and found themselves in a wonderland. Brocade chairs, tapestry carpets, carved ivory tables, fine glass, paintings and silk wall hangings made the cave a palace. Diamonds, hanging on chains from the ceiling, twinkled brightly in the lantern light. Gold ingots stacked like bricks gleamed from the walls. A chest of emeralds lay beside a bed studded with pearls and amber, and covered in silken sheets. Bags of pepper, cinnamon, cloves and nutmeg scented the air.

"We're in Aladdin's cave!" said Al.

"Look over there," said Jack. "There's a bath made of gold and it's full of dried puffer fish! Isn't that the weirdest thing you've ever seen?"

"Puffer fish?" said Al. "I think I read somewhere that puffer fish are poisonous. In the olden days witchdoctors made potions out of the poison, which turned people into mindless zombies. Do you think that's what Velvetfoot is doing?"

"It must be! There's lots of jars and a fireplace over there," said Jack, pointing to the back of the cave.

Along with the jars they found bottles filled with strange chemicals and more puffer fish that had been cut into tiny pieces.

"So this is where Velvetfoot makes his zombie brew," said Al. "At least we know what he's doing, but I'm not sure that will help Blacktooth, because even if we destroy this store, Velvetfoot knows how to make more."

"I think we should just do everything we can to get off this island," said Jack. He held out a ruby necklace hanging on a strong chain. "We could lash some wood together and use some of this strong jewellery to make a raft."

"It's worth a try," said Al. "Velvetfoot said the currents brought him ships, so there has to be a strong current nearby and a shipping lane. We might find someone passing through who'll rescue us and we could pay our way with the jewels."

"There's food in here," said Jack, peering into a large barrel. "We could take supplies, too."

Desperate to escape, the boys scoured the beach for logs and driftwood. Before long they had built a small raft tied together with jewellery taken from Velvetfoot's treasure. Jack also found some spare galley oars. Using one as a mast, another as a tiller, and some of the silk sheets as a sail, they set off with the tide.

The jewelled raft drifted into the ocean. Al kept an eye on the sun and noticed that the current took them west.

That night, as the seas were calm, the boys took it in turns sleeping. In the morning, still heading west and with the wind behind them, they hoisted their sail. During the day they sighted a ship's sail but, as hard as they called and waved, it passed them by.

They were starting to feel like they'd be stranded for ever. But, late in the afternoon, as Al squinted into the sun, Jack saw a boat sailing rapidly towards them from the east, its copper hull reflecting the sun's light. He let out a cheer and Al turned their raft and tacked back towards Captain Gunner's boat, *The Invincible*.

Explaining to Gunner

"Blacktooth's a mindless zombie!" chortled Gunner, slapping his thighs and shaking with laughter. "A zombie! Oh, you boys have made my day!" He pulled a ruby pendant from the boy's raft, which had been hauled onto *The Invincible*'s deck. "And you not only bring good news; you've brought me a treasure fit for a king!" He draped the pendant over the neck of a white, three-legged cat who had made himself at home on the raft. "This is your share, Snakeboot," he said to the ship's cat. "And Blacktooth's never gunner worry us again!"

"We always said you boys were lucky," said Mozzy, the bosun.

"And I'll have this," said Slicer, the cook, holding up a chain with a diamond that glinted in the sun.

"Where did you go, anyway?" asked Mahoot, the cabin boy. "It's been ages since you left us and I've missed you."

"And where's the scabbard and sabre?" asked Gunner, his mind snapping away from Blacktooth's problems. "Have you left them with your sister again?"

Al nodded. "They're in the same place," he answered. "But we didn't use the sabre to get here. We haven't learned how to use it yet."

Gunner's smile disappeared. "There's no reason to lie to me," he complained. "If you boys and I are gunner remain friends you have to tell the truth. You must know how the sabre works. How else can you always come up with treasure? No one else can do that."

Al shrugged his shoulders. It was no use trying to explain how they had arrived on Velvetfoot's boat, because Gunner's mind was made up that the sabre was working again and was somehow responsible for them leaping from place to place.

Jack decided it was time to change the subject, so he focused on Gunner's other favourite topic. "The treasure in the cave we found is amazing – there are diamonds hanging from the roof!"

At the word 'treasure' a glint came to Gunner's eyes. "Do you think you could find Velvetfoot's island again?" he asked.

Al nodded. "We were carried by the current for one day and we sailed with the wind today, so the island must be due east of here, but I don't know how fast the current is or how far we drifted."

"There's no island on my maps," said Gunner thoughtfully. "Around here all that's shown is this big fast current."

"Well, it's not a very big island," said Jack, "and it was a day's row from where a warning bell sat on some rocks and where Velvetfoot caught Blacktooth."

"Ah, that'd be Big Boomer," said Gunner.

"That bell's saved many a mariner for more than thirty years." He did a quick calculation. "If the zombies rowed for a day, and you drifted and sailed for two days, and the speed of the current is…" His face lit up and he turned to Mozzy. "Set sail and hold a course at twenty-two degrees east."

Attack of the Zombies

Meanwhile, Velvetfoot had found something disturbing. Frustrated, he turned to a nearby skull.

"Zombies don't eat," he said, "but my biscuits have gone, so someone's been hidin' on my boat. Velvetfoot's been lazy. He should've counted how many men he rescued. Velvetfoot should've watched each man swallow the potion!" He turned to

Blacktooth. "One of yer crew is out and about and Velvetfoot is angry with ye."

Worrying that someone had, somehow, hidden on his galley and later escaped, he ordered the zombie crew to turn the boat about and row back to the island. And once inside his cave he discovered the missing sheets, oars and treasure. He punched the air angrily, his ancient blood boiling in fury.

"Thief! Robber!" he shouted. "I'll find ye and roast yer gizzards in a fire!"

He sent his zombies to search the island thoroughly. When they returned empty-handed, Velvetfoot's pale eyes narrowed. "So ye've escaped me," he grumbled. "But Velvetfoot knows the mind of men, and ye have seen a richness so great ye'll return. And ye'll bring others to help ye plunder Velvetfoot's treasure, but Velvetfoot'll be ready and waitin' for ye."

Velvetfoot made himself busy. First the

zombies dug a bearpit in the middle of the
track leading to his cave. Velvetfoot covered
the pit in fabric and disguised it with leaves
and sand. He gave the men ropes and they
pulled his flat-bottomed slave galleon into
shore and camouflaged it with leaves. Then
he armed his strongest zombies, including
Blacktooth and Pigface, and placed them
in a hiding spot near the track. Finally, the
smaller crew members were sent to watch for
anyone's arrival.

"Like flies in jam," Velvetfoot said with a
smirk. "I'll have them all in my trap."

And knowing the zombies would watch
day and night without sleep or food,
Velvetfoot tucked himself into his beautiful
bed and slept like a baby.

Meanwhile, Gunner tacked back and forth
on the edge of the current. Just on sundown,
Mahoot spied a coconut floating in the

waves and Mozzy saw
some birds.

"There's an island
around here, no doubt,"
said Gunner, "but she
must be low-lying and
a bit further east."

The ship continued
its course until the
following morning. The
sunlight shimmered
oddly on the horizon
and Gunner knew they
had found what they
were looking for. They
struck anchor a long
way from the island and
lowered the longboat.
"We're gunner row
ashore so no one sees
our sail," said Gunner.

With Al and Jack directing them, Gunner's pirates made their way through the bushes towards the track leading to the treasure cave.

Once on the path, the eager pirates rushed forward, leaving Al, Jack and Mahoot to fall behind. They hadn't gone far when Al glimpsed something yellow, off to one side, among the trees. Suspicious, he left the group to investigate and Jack and Mahoot followed him.

As they got closer they found Flash Johnny staring out to sea, keeping watch, but, being a zombie, he only looked in one direction, so he hadn't heard the boys sneaking up from behind. Realising he might turn at any moment, the boys launched themselves forward, grabbed him in a rugby tackle and brought him to the ground. They removed their belts and bound him hand and foot so he couldn't get to Velvetfoot and raise the alarm.

"We'll have to hurry and warn Gunner that Velvetfoot is back on the island and he's set a watch," said Al. "We can come back and release Flash later."

As they raced back through the bush, the shouts of fighting men and the clashing of metal on metal warned the boys they were too late. They dropped down and

crawled forward cautiously to see what was happening.

Gunner's men were fighting valiantly against a heavily armed foe. Gunner's face was covered in blood from a gash on his forehead and more dripped from nasty wounds along Mozzy's arm. Slicer was slashing at his opponents with a sharp knife. His fast thrusts

and jabs inflicted terrible injuries but, to his horror, didn't cause the wounds to bleed.

As the zombies didn't appear to feel any pain, they pushed Gunner's men backwards along the track, oblivious to their injuries, while several of Gunner's pirates fell under their vicious attack.

Finally the unstoppable foe was too much. Gunner's crew lost their courage, dropped their weapons and ran for their lives.

The boys followed, keeping their friends in sight, hoping for an opportunity to help them.

But just before the treasure cave, Gunner's men tumbled into the bearpit trap. Velvetfoot emerged from the trees, smiling. With his blunderbuss pointed down into the pit, he ordered one of his zombies to lower a blue bottle down to *The Invincible*'s crew. "Drink or die where you are!" he shouted, cocking the gun.

That night, as the moon rose, Gunner and his men were pulled from the bearpit as zombies. The remnants of Blacktooth's crew also drank from the blue bottle, and the mortally wounded zombies, who could not drink, finally fell dead where they stood.

There, under the rocky overhang, those remaining sat, silent and unmoving, waiting for Velvetfoot to give them instructions. But Velvetfoot went into his cave, closed the door and went to bed.

The boys decided to leave their hiding place and walk along the beach. "Flash'll be awake by now," said Al, "because the zombie brew will have worn off. He'll be really uncomfortable and we can't leave him like that."

"We'll have to guard him and think of a way to help our friends at the same time," grumbled Jack. "He'll be a real pain and he won't want to help us, I'm sure."

"Ouch!" cried Mahoot, as he tumbled with a thud into the sand. He struggled to get up. Jack and Al rushed over to him. His foot was caught in something. They pulled away, realising he was tangled in the edge of a fishing net.

As they freed Mahoot's foot, Al said, "Let's pull the rest of the net out of the sand."

"Why?" asked Jack.

"I want to see if it's big enough to make a trap," replied Al, hauling one edge. It was well buried, but the three of them soon exposed a strong fishing net more than three metres long and nearly as wide.

"There's a small hole in it," said Al, inspecting their find, "but not big enough to let a man escape."

"How could we use it?" asked Mahoot. "Velvetfoot's in his cave. Could we sneak in and throw it over him while he's sleeping?"

"He'd hear the levers click as the door opened," said Al, as he tested the net's weight.

"And I don't think we're tall or strong enough to do it quickly and restrain him." He sat down in the sand and thought for a while before continuing. "But the controls for the cave door are under trees," he said. "Maybe we could climb into the branches, spread the net and drop it on him when he goes to close the door, then jump down and wrap him up!"

"It's worth a try," Mahoot agreed. "We can't let Captain Gunner and the crew be taken away on the slave galley."

"They'll probably leave first thing in the morning," said Jack. "Can we rig the net in the dark?"

"We'll have to try," said Al. "And we'll have to start now. That means we have to leave Flash where he is, but it's worth the risk, otherwise we'll *all* be zombies."

The following morning the boys lay along the tree branches, nervously holding their net and

waiting for Velvetfoot to stand beside
his levers.

The man eventually appeared, carrying
a blue bottle, and gave each zombie a drink.
By the time he'd finished, the boys' arms
were aching with the weight of the net. Al
almost let out a loud sigh of frustration when
Velvetfoot, still angry about being robbed,
began to shout at his new captives.

"Ye've given Velvetfoot a bad time!" he
ranted. "So ye'll be made to row further and
harder than any of Velvetfoot's other crews.
Velvetfoot'll make ye sorry ye were ever born.
Ye will all die a painful death for causing me
so much trouble." He lifted Blacktooth's head.
"And yer head will not hang with the others.
Ye be no friend of mine."

During the tirade, a flash of yellow moving
among the bushes behind Velvetfoot's back
caught Al's eye. To his horror he realised Flash
had escaped! His arrival might ruin their plan.

Sure enough, seconds later, Flash darted from the bushes, wielding Slicer's sharp cooking knife. He plunged it into Velvetfoot's back.

Shock lit the deathless pirate's eyes. He staggered, turned, and saw Flash, a grim smile playing on his lips. "Scurvy pup! I'd forgotten ye even existed. Velvetfoot's making too many mistakes. But ye'll not live long." He reached over his shoulder, grabbed the hilt of the knife and pulled it from his back.

Stunned and disbelieving, Flash stood rooted to the spot as Velvetfoot leapt towards him.

Flash recovered just in time, took to his heels and fled for his life.

"Now what?" said Mahoot. "We can't stay up here all day. My arms'll give out!"

"The island's small," said Al. "Flash'll run around for a bit and come back looking for another weapon. He probably thinks Velvetfoot is wearing some sort of vest that stopped the knife from hurting him. I think we should stay where we are a bit longer."

Sure enough, Flash had doubled back and, seeing the secret door in the rocks wide open, dashed inside.

"He'll faint when he sees all the treasure," said Jack.

Several minutes later Flash emerged, carrying Velvetfoot's blunderbuss. He sat down directly beneath the boys, held his gun level, and waited for Velvetfoot's return. The boys waited above him, barely daring to breathe, their arms aching.

Several tense minutes went by before Velvetfoot returned, and spotting Flash's bright jacket, strode towards him.

"There's no escape from this island!" Velvetfoot shouted. "And I'll take pleasure in wringing yer stinkin' neck!"

With a mighty boom, Flash fired the blunderbuss. The recoil knocked him backwards and his shot went wide of the mark.

Velvetfoot, eyes glittering with fury, charged towards Flash before he could reload.

Flash, fearing his end had come, and trapped under the rocky overhang, rolled onto his stomach and screamed for mercy.

As Velvetfoot lunged for the kill, the boys dropped their net. It hit its mark and they leapt from their hiding place, landing beside Velvetfoot.

Velvetfoot struggled against the webbing, but the boys grabbed the net's edges and ran around him, wrapping him up before he could escape.

Flash, his face buried in the earth, howled in terror as the boys struggled with the deathless pirate.

Although Velvetfoot was entangled in the net, his knife hand was free and he ruthlessly thrust and cut at the boys. The faster the boys dodged and moved, the faster again the ancient pirate turned, the knife whipping through the air. Al ducked as the blade whistled past his ear, narrowly missing his neck. Jack caught a cut to his jacket and only just managed to pull back before he was wounded. Mahoot leapt high, dodging a stab to the thigh.

Al finally got both hands on the net and yanked hard, toppling Velvetfoot. The pirate rolled over and over, dragging the boys with him as he gripped the mesh, slicing at their hands to loosen their grasp.

The boys jumped up quickly, darting in and out, twisting the net ever tighter. Suddenly, Velvetfoot changed his tactic and slashed at the threads with the knife. Jack realised he would be free in seconds and looked around for something to help them.

A stout branch lay on the ground. He grabbed it and, holding it above his head, brought it down with all his might, hitting the knife out of Velvetfoot's grasp, landing beside Flash.

Having disarmed the pirate, the boys

continued to wrap him tightly. Finally, when Velvetfoot was trapped and unable to move, the boys sat on him, pinning him to the ground.

"Now what?" said Al. "What shall we do with him?"

All this time Flash had moaned in fear, and he hadn't looked up once. When he finally realised all was quiet, he came to his senses. He sat up, with tears still trickling down his face, staring in surprise at the scene.

In front of him, sitting on the now motionless Velvetfoot, were Al, Jack and Mahoot, his most hated enemies. His first instinct was to face the horrible pirate who had nearly killed him. He leapt to his feet and grabbed the abandoned knife, meaning to rush upon the fallen victim and stab him. But as he did so, he realised that the boys had heard his terrified screams and probably seen his tears, and his fear turned to anger. His face hardened and his eyes flashed defiance and aggression. He swaggered towards the boys, knife pointed directly at them.

"You stinking chunder-buckets aren't getting my treasure!" he shouted. "I'm taking it all." He kicked out at Al, and put his foot on Velvetfoot's chest. "Everything this pirate has is mine, and before I kill him, I'll take a trophy to remember him by."

Flash reached down and pulled Velvetfoot's ring from his hand.

"Don't do that!" cried Al, grabbing at Flash to stop him from taking the black diamond ring.

"You're not having it," said Flash angrily, slashing out with his knife. "It's mine!" he bragged, as he ripped the ring from Velvetfoot's finger.

At the same time an eerie, drawn-out scream erupted from Velvetfoot's throat. It shivered the leaves on the trees and sent goosebumps down the boys' spines. Flash froze, his hand just above Velvetfoot's.

The deathless pirate's hand twisted upwards, the tendons shrinking, making a claw. His sharp fingernails hooked into Flash's skin. Flash tried to tear his hand away, but Velvetfoot's ancient fingers were ripped from his crumbling hand and clung to the boy. Shrieking in terror at the sight, he leapt up and down, furiously shaking his hand to free himself from the rotten flesh and, in so doing, flinging the stolen ring into the bushes.

The ancient pirate went rigid, his face changed colour and a dark, almost orange, smoke oozed from his nostrils and ears.

"What's happening?" cried Flash fearfully, as Velvetfoot's body began to convulse. "Is he a devil? Is he going to get me?"

Before Al could even think to answer, Velvetfoot's jaw disintegrated, his eyes bulged

outwards and popped
and his body hissed
and melted. Seconds
later he had vanished
altogether.

Flash, gasping in
horror, began to pace
up and down, trying to
calm himself. Finally
he remembered his
enemies, so stepped
forward, slashing the
knife through the
air. "I'll slit your gizzards now!" he shouted
nervously. "All the treasure here's mine and
you can't have it!"

Al stepped back. "Flash, we saved your life.
You owe us one and you know it."

Flash looked a little taken aback. He
lowered the knife slightly.

Al realised that he was talking to a bully,

so he needed to trick him. He had to make him feel that he was in charge. He put on a scared face. "You're bigger and stronger than us," he said. "All we want is to go free. You and your shipmates can have everything inside the cave. That's a pirate's promise." He spat on his hand, holding it out, waiting for Flash to calm down.

"I can cut you in a second," said Flash, eyeing Al suspiciously. "We know when we've had enough," said Al, letting his bottom lip quiver. "That disgusting pirate, exploding like that, really scared us." Flash smiled, showing his white teeth. Cockily, he stepped forward, spat on his hand and shook.

Al pointed to the cave. "It's all yours. All we want to do is take our friends back to the boat. You've got so much treasure now, you can be king of the world."

"Yes," said Jack, picking up on Al's train of thought. "And I want to go home to my mum." He wiped an imaginary tear from his eye.

Seeing the miserable boys, Flash felt confident he wouldn't have any more trouble from them. "Bunch of sooks," he mocked. "I can't stand to look at little sooks. You're not even worth killing." He flashed an arrogant smile at Al, then turned, eager to get away from the memory of devilish crumbling pirates and to go and count his gold and diamonds.

"You get off the island and take your friends with you!" he shouted down the tunnel. "Be gone in an hour. If one of you comes near me, I'll skewer you."

The black diamond ring he had ripped from

Velvetfoot's hand was long forgotten.

Al gave him ten seconds, then leapt towards the levers under the trees and pulled them. With a grinding clunk the door swung shut, trapping Flash inside.

"Phew!" said Jack.

"It'll take him for ever to work out how to get out," laughed Al. "He's not too good at codes."

Mahoot bent and picked up Velvetfoot's black diamond ring. "Look," he said, "it's not inside the cave, so it isn't part of your pirate's oath. You can take it."

The Final Resting Place

At sunset the boys picked up Velvetfoot's blue bottle. They went to each of Blacktooth's crew and gave them a drink.

"That will make them stay zombies for a while longer and give us a chance to escape without a fight," said Al, making sure Blacktooth had an extra mouthful.

"And what do you think Flash will do when he gets out of the cave?" asked Mahoot.

"If the other pirates are awake, he won't be

able to do anything," replied Al. "But if he gets out before then, he might keep them as zombies. There's a lot of potion still in the cave, although he doesn't know the recipe."

As he spoke, Gunner yawned and stretched. He looked around, bewildered. "Glad you're with us," said Al. "We've got work to do, and we have to get back to *The Invincible* as soon as everyone's returned to normal."

When they arrived back at the longboat, Jack stopped. "I wouldn't want Flash and Blacktooth to take the galley out, capture another ship and turn more men into zombies," he said. "I think we should sink the galley and give all those poor captains a sea burial."

"I agree," said Gunner. "We'll row around and tow it out to sea."

Several hours later, just on dusk, the galley was alongside *The Invincible*, and Gunner was pouring a barrel of oil into its hull. The boys were also aboard the galley, chopping down the cabin and making a pyre of wood. When all was ready, Gunner set a slow fuse into some gunpowder and lit its end, before he and the boys beat a speedy retreat to *The Invincible*.

Once they were safely on board, Gunner ordered the galley cast off and it drifted away towards the sunset.

As the flames lit the night sky, the pirates leant on *The Invincible* rails in silence. "All those poor old captains are gunner go to their rest down in Davey Jones's Locker," said Gunner.

"I'm grateful to you boys for not letting us die as zombies," said Slicer.

"There are fates worse than death," Gunner agreed.

"Blacktooth will be very wealthy after this," said Mozzy. "That really burns me gall bladder!"

"But he'll be rich pickings," Gunner said with a smile. "I'm gunner make his life miserable. Every time he sails out to spend a bit of what he's got, I'll be there waiting for

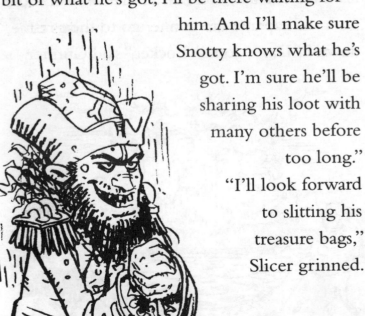

him. And I'll make sure Snotty knows what he's got. I'm sure he'll be sharing his loot with many others before too long."

"I'll look forward to slitting his treasure bags," Slicer grinned.

With the flames from the burning galley still brightening the night sky, Mahoot said, "There are no more deathless pirates left in the Dragon Blood Islands. Things will be quiet."

"Al, you have all the diamonds for the Scabbard of Invincibility now," said Gunner. "And I'll bet that means you're gunner disappear off somewhere again as soon as we get to town."

"But when you do, make sure you bring us back more treasure, like you did this time," said Mozzy.

Return of the Scabbard's Powers

Once they were back in town, Snakeboot
jumped ship and led the boys to Alleric
Warehouse. At the door, after nodding to Jack
in silent agreement, Al turned to Mahoot.
"We're going home now," he told his friend.
"We live somewhere else and Snakeboot
sometimes takes us home from this
warehouse. We don't know how he knows

when or where to do it, but it just happens and we don't seem to have much say in it. We promise you we'll come back soon."

Mahoot smiled. "I understand," he said. "Snakeboot's magical. Ever since Vicious Victor told us that cat was here to help you, I knew you had come from somewhere strange. But I know you'll come back with the scabbard, and I hope you'll use it to help us restore Sabre Island, make Grandfather happy and keep the elephants safe."

"We will," said Al. "I promise. I'll go home and put the last diamond in the scabbard. Then we'll come back. I'm sorry you can't come with us. I hope you understand."

Mahoot nodded. "You're my best friends," he said. "I'll always trust you."

The boys shook hands and, with Snakeboot leading them, left Mahoot and entered the warehouse. Once inside and out of sight, they felt a familiar tingle in their legs. Al saw that

Jack had begun to shimmer brightly and become transparent, and seconds later they found themselves back in the attic at number five Drake Drive in the twenty-first century. Once again, Snakeboot was with them. There was the wonderful smell of a baking cake, the phone was ringing and Al's sister Hally was singing loudly to her MP3 player.

"Horrible noise," said Jack. "Worse than Velvetfoot's death scream."

Al smiled and held up the black diamond ring. "Come back tomorrow," he said. "We'll put the diamond in the scabbard and see if it's true that whoever wears it becomes invincible."

Captain's Code

The codes on pages 41 and 42 are written in 'second-letter code'. To decipher them, ignore every second letter – this will give you the first part of the message. Then go back and read the letters that were skipped to get the second part of the message.

Check out www.dragonbloodpirates.co.uk for clues to the Captain's Code…if you dare!

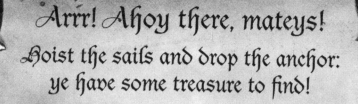

Arrr! Ahoy there, mateys!
Hoist the sails and drop the anchor: ye have some treasure to find!

One swashbucklin' reader will win an ipod Touch and ten runners up will win a Dragon Blood Pirates booty bag. For a chance to win, ye must dare to unearth the treasure!

Each of the six **Dragon Blood Pirates: The Legend of Dragon Island** books contain a clue. When you have solved the six clues, enter the answers online at www.dragonbloodpirates.co.uk

Or send your name, address and answers to:

Dragon Blood Pirates:
The Legend of Dragon Island
338 Euston Road, London NW1 3BH

Best o' luck, me hearties!

To find where the pirate treasure lies,
ye must find the answer to the clue that lies below:

**This boat rescues our heroes stuck on a raft,
As they escape from a pirate with
a sleeping draught.**

Only one entry per child. Final draw 31 August 2011.
For full terms and conditions visit
www.dragonbloodpirates.co.uk/terms

www.dragonbloodpirates.co.uk

Ahoy there shipmates!

To reel in amazin' pirate booty, steer smartly
towards www.dragonbloodpirates.co.uk

Ye'll find games, downloads, activities and
sneak previews of the latest swashbucklin'
Dragon Blood Pirates adventures.
Learn how to speak all pirate-like, how to find
out what type of pirate ye be, an' what pirate
games ye can play with yer mates! This treasure
trove is a sure feast fer yer deadlights!

Only the bravest an' heartiest amon' ye
can become a true scurvy dog, so don't
ye miss a thing and sign up to yer newsletter
at www.dragonbloodpirates.co.uk!

Don't ye miss book twelve in the
Dragon Blood Pirates
series!

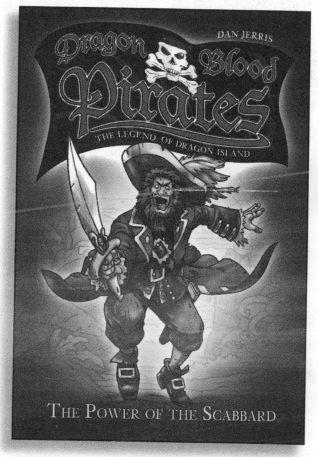

Turn the page and shiver yer timbers
with a slice of the next high-seas adventure...

Invincible

Alleric Breas had just finished polishing the Scabbard of Invincibility when his best friend, Jack Seabrook, bounced happily into the attic. Al held the scabbard up to show Jack – its four black diamonds glittered on the silver mesh.

Jack picked up the Dragon Blood Sabre, which was beside Al, and swished it through the air. "Wow! Don't they both look great?" he said.

Snakeboot, their white, three-legged cat,

purred loudly in approval from the lid of an old sea trunk.

Jack reached out to touch the scabbard. "Does it work?"

Al shrugged. "I wouldn't like to test it. To do that I'd have to try and injure myself."

"But we could try something easy," suggested Jack. "I could stick a pin in your finger and see if it makes a mark."

Al reached into a cupboard drawer, rummaged around, found a pin and held it out. Jack gave Al's hand a quick jab. To his surprise the pin bent, and Al's finger was untouched.

"Wow!" the boys said together. Then they rushed downstairs to the bathroom, ran the hot tap and Al stuck his finger under it. He didn't feel the hot water at all. "It works," he chortled. "It really works! I'm invincible!"

They returned to the attic where Snakeboot leapt from the trunk. He sunk his claws into Al's arm.

"Not a scratch," smiled Al, reaching down to pat the cat. "Thanks, Snakeboot."

Snakeboot purred and leapt back onto the trunk, but this time he clawed the lid. "Are you saying it's time to go?" asked Jack.

"We'd better change into our pirate clothes," said Al. "This time I hope we land on Sabre Island so we can show Mahoot's grandfather that we've got the scabbard working."

Minutes later the boys were dressed and eagerly following Snakeboot into Al's grandfather's sea trunk. Al focused on the map of the Dragon Blood Islands drawn in the bottom, and especially on Sabre Island. As he wished himself there, his arms and legs began to tingle. He saw his friend Jack begin to shimmer and dissolve, and both boys left number five Drake Drive and the twenty-first century.

Cobra

Al and Jack found themselves in a familiar pergola. "We're in the summer house on Sabre Island," said Al, looking around. He opened a creaky old door and stepped outside into a bird-filled jungle.

As they made their way down to a nearby creek, voices carried to the boys through the trees. "Put your backs into it! I've got two hogsheads to fill by tonight's tide."

"That's Mozzy bossing the crew around," said Al, quickening his pace, with Snakeboot bounding behind him.

They soon came across *The Invincible*'s crew filling water barrels in the sun. Captain Gunner was sitting in the shade of a large tree and, seeing the boys, leapt to his feet.

"You're back!" he cried. "And you've brought Snakeboot too. We've missed him!"

A bare-footed boy turned and rushed towards his friends.

"Mahoot!" said Al and Jack together.

"You've repaired the scabbard," said Gunner, eyeing the glittering weapon. "That's great. I'm sure we're gunner get lots of treasure now!"

Jack laughed. Gunner's first thought was always of treasure. "Before we go treasure hunting," he said, "we want to see Mahoot's grandfather."

"He'll be so happy," said Mahoot. "He still dreams of Sabre Island being a safe place again."

"Why don't we sit down for a few minutes before you rush off?" suggested Gunner. "I'd love to look at your treasures. You can tell me how you got the sabre working again and how it brought you here."

Al and Jack sat down with Gunner under the tree. "We haven't actually got the sabre working," Jack tried to explain. "If Al had managed that, how could he have got Snakeboot and me here too? There's other magic happening and we just haven't worked it out properly yet."

"Well," said Gunner, "I can understand you don't want folk believing the sabre's working." He touched his nose and winked. "But you can trust me. I'll tell everyone else it's not working. I was just hoping you were gunner tell me the—"

His words were interrupted by a growl from Snakeboot. The cat's fur stood on end, his back arched threateningly and his purple eyes glared at something next to Gunner.

A large cobra reared from the bushes, its hood flaring, poised and ready to strike. Behind it several smaller cobras squirmed aggressively.

"It's a nest!" shouted Jack. "We're sitting on a cobra's nest!"

"Don't move!" cried Al. But his warning was of no use because Gunner, seeing the snake, let out a yell and leapt away. Unfortunately, his feet tangled, making him fall, his frantic movements attracting the cobras.

Without thinking, Al threw himself between Gunner and the snakes just as they slithered forward. Covered in cobras, Al rolled on the ground. The smaller snakes clung to his jacket and wrapped around his legs, while the large one struck at his neck. Finally, Al stopped moving and sat up, slightly stunned, with the snakes writhing angrily

around him. Poison dripped from his jacket
and breeches, but not a drop had gone into
his skin. Ashen-faced, he pulled the snakes
off and threw them into the jungle. The crew
of *The Invincible* stood around him, staring in
awe.

"The scabbard has saved you," said
Gunner. "And you saved me!"

"That's amazing," said Slicer, the cook. "If
I hadn't seen it, I'd not believe it!"

"It really works!" cried Mahoot. "This is
the best news ever!"

But as Al looked around at his friends, he

wasn't so sure. Gunner's eyes had a hint of jealousy and Slicer's eyes held greed. I must remember they're pirates, he thought, but then he shook the thought away. Gunner was his friend, after all, and there was a pirate code! Al was sure he was safe with his shipmates.

Later that night, the boys sat around Mahoot's grandfather's table and, after they had enjoyed a delicious meal of saffron rice and jungle vegetables, Al put the sabre and scabbard on the table for the old man to see.

Strangely, Mahoot's grandfather didn't touch them. He looked at Al sadly.

"Now, young Prince Alleric," he said, "thank you for finding these treasures and offering them to me. Unfortunately I cannot take them yet. Despite all your hard work, the magical words that give the sabre its strength have not yet been found. Without those

words you cannot come and go as you please.
I am old, but I know I will live till you find
those words and restore the sabre's powers.
Until then, you must keep these weapons
and continue your search. With their return,
however, dangerous times begin for you.
Every man will want them. Remember to
keep one eye open, even when you sleep.
There are perils outside the jungle and there
is a poison in men's hearts that causes more
damage than any snake."

The Lure of Treasure

After a day on Sabre Island, where they swam with the elephants and visited the elephant's graveyard with Mahoot's grandfather, Al and Jack set sail with Gunner at sunset and headed for town.

The following day Gunner went ashore to spy on other captains' sailing plans and what they might be carrying. "There might be a load of silk we can steal, or a hold of spices," he said to Mozzy, the bosun. "There have been very few pickings leaving town lately."

Left alone, Al, Jack and Mahoot enjoyed watching the hustle and bustle of the crowded port from the decks of *The Invincible,* until Gunner returned later in the afternoon and called them over.

"I've got an errand for you," he said. "My compass is broken." He handed Al some gold pieces. "I'd like you to go over to Stanley Spong's and buy a good second-hand one."

As the boys and Snakeboot went to disembark, Gunner called out, "I wouldn't take the sabre and scabbard with you. You'll be robbed!"

"He's right," agreed Jack. "Put them in our cabin. We won't be long."

An hour later, carrying a brass compass and feeling pleased that they had got the best possible price from Spong, the boys returned to the docks. Snakeboot bounded ahead, but as they approached the wharf where *The Invincible* had berthed, they found it empty.

"Have we got the wrong quay?" asked Jack, bewildered.

"Snakeboot never makes mistakes," said Al, staring uncomfortably at the empty mooring lines rolled neatly on the jetty.

"Then Gunner's gone without us," said Mahoot, disbelieving. "Unless his ship was hijacked."

"What will we do?" said Jack. "We've got nowhere to stay."

"But more importantly, where on earth has it gone and how will we find it?" asked Al, shocked.

What the boys didn't know was that Gunner had returned from town with some very interesting news. Blacktooth was back! The gossip was that he had recently rowed into town in a patched-up longboat. He had brought with him a casket of gold and purchased a well-found barque which he had renamed *The Tyrant*. He'd fitted it out with ten cannon and set sail. It was rumoured that he was planning to return to buy another ship, load it with timber and build a fort on some secret island.

The news was too much for Gunner. He knew which island Blacktooth was living on and how he had ended up with the treasure of Velvetfoot, the deathless pirate. That treasure, he told himself, should have been his. If it hadn't been for those children making a deal with Blacktooth's cabin boy, Flash, then the treasure would be sitting in Gunner's hold.

I'm gunner attack Blacktooth and take his gold as he sails into town, thought Gunner as he made his way back to his ship. I'm gunner sail this afternoon and wait for him near that group of small islands I know about. I'll spring out with all guns firing. *The Invincible's* got long-range cannons, so he's got no chance. But we'll have to board *The Tyrant* and Blacktooth's a dirty fighter. If I had the

Scabbard of Invincibility I'd beat him in a minute.

Once back on *The Invincible*, Gunner went to his cabin and brooded. He knew the boys wouldn't let him have the scabbard. But, if they weren't around, and the scabbard was just lying in their cabin…

And before he knew what he was doing, Gunner had left the boys on their errand and set sail without them.

War of Words

Gunner sailed to a group of small islands that lay beside a fast current the merchantmen used to navigate into town. There was only one safe anchorage and it was very small, but it hid any ship from sight. It was the perfect place to launch an attack on a passing vessel. All Gunner had to do was set a watch on the headland and, when the signal was given that Blacktooth's barque was sighted, set sail into the current and cut him off.

As dusk fell, Gunner, with the last of the

wind, forced *The Invincible* against the current and slid into the anchorage. To his horror, a worn-out old West Indiaman was already moored in his spot.

"It's Snotty!" he grumbled. "What's she doing here? Could she have found out about Blacktooth's treasure and be setting an ambush too?"

Meanwhile, Snotty Nell and her daughter, Grenda, were sitting on the poop deck of the *Nausi VIII*, and Snotty was enjoying her favourite drink, sahlep tea. She was doing her best, as usual, not to look over the side of the boat into the water, because circling below was a huge white pointer shark, Greeny Joe.

Snotty's nerves were on edge. Her temper was raw and unsettled and she was very worried. Her first mate, Vampire Zu, had just given her some bad news…